Imagination Song

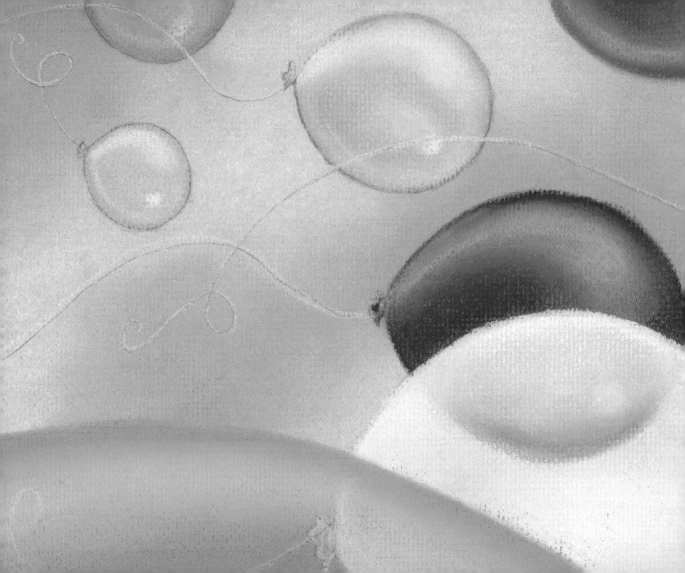

With much love to my parents, Hilda & Phil.
Also to Cheryl Henson.
—L.L.

Library of Congress Cataloging-in-Publication Data
Raposo, Joe.
Imagination song / by Joe Raposo ; illustrated by Laurent Linn. p. cm.
SUMMARY: An illustrated version of this song celebrating the imagination.
ISBN 0-375-80688-1 (trade) — ISBN 0-375-90688-6 (lib. bdg.)
1. Children's songs—Texts. [1. Imagination—Songs and music. 2. Songs.] I. Linn, Laurent, ill. II. Title.
PZ8.3.R1765 Im 2001   782.42164'0268—dc21   [E]   00-068325

www.randomhouse.com/kids/sesame
www.sesamestreet.com

Printed in Italy   October 2001   10 9 8 7 6 5 4 3 2 1
First Edition

Imagination Song

By Joe Raposo

Illustrated by Laurent Linn

Random House New York

Here, in the middle of imagination

right in the middle of my head . . .

I close my eyes and my home isn't home . . .

and my bed isn't really my bed.

I look inside and discover things
that are sometimes strange and new.

And the most remarkable thoughts I think
have a way of being true.

Here, in the middle of imagination,
right in the middle of my mind . . .

I close my eyes and the night isn't dark . . .

and the things that I lose, I find.

Time stands still . . .

and the night is clear . . .

and the wind is warm and fair.

And the nicest place is the middle of imagination when I'm there.

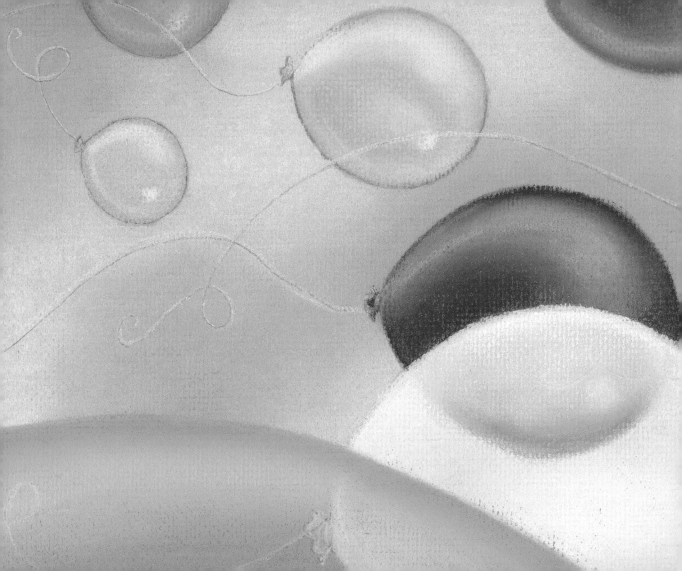